Chronicles of the Seventh Realm: River of Blood

Chronicles of the Seventh Realm

River of Blood

Scroll 1

Rose Sweetwater

CHRONICLES OF THE SEVENTH REALM

Rose Sweetwater Publishing
4897 Bennetts Pasture Rd. Unit 5310
Suffolk VA 23435

www.rosesweetwater.com

https://www.facebook.com/authorrose

Library of Congress Publication date is available upon request.

ISBN-13: 978-0-9916486-0-3
ISBN-10: 0991648609

For Joseph,
My anchor, I love you.

CONTENTS

ACKNOWLEDGEMENTS

There are not enough words to express my gratitude to all who have contributed to the success of this work, but I will start with this… Thank you. Your confidence and vision in my ability and strength, even when I lacked the courage and will, has proven invaluable.

To the Universal Mind, that God mind within and about me: I say thank you. I am humbled and grateful to know you.

To my parents: a big fat hug, a billion kisses, and more thank you's than I can express…yes Abah Leeveel that means you too…

To my husband and children: Thank you for putting up with me, and believing in me.

To my family both named and unnamed, I thank you. To my SL friends and those I call family, named and unnamed, I thank you; LONG LIVE SEVARDI.

To the sweetest girl a person could ever know, hence the nickname Sweet Pea… Thank you girl, your inspiration means the world to me.

To Desire: a beacon of joy, love, hope and light; a friend, sister, and mother, I say thank you.

To Anaviel: what can I say… you rock. Thank you.

To Kris & Clia, Marcus & Vella, Ari, James, Ben and a very special Kitty: I thank you.

To the CreateSpace team, your guidance has been invaluable; thank you.

To my editor Kristen House, I cannot say enough to express my gratitude. So I will start with thank you. You are a blessing, and your eyes are like magic. I am grateful for your professionalism and attention to detail. I would also like to add: "You're stuck with me now."

INTRODUCTION

Welcome to the Chronicles. Created as a window into the seventh realm, these scrolls will help you better understand the individual lives and contributions of the characters within the seventh realm work. Scroll one offers a brief history into the realm, and its primary fashions. *River of Blood* explores the life of Benjamin with a brief overview of his past, while pinpointing major contributions he has made to the realms in which he is forced to call home. There are many realms or dimensions parallel to our own, and although time moves differently in each one of them, the realm of Earth is unique, and is the ultimate prize as far as Benjamin is concerned— simply because it is the closest to his ancestral home than any other realm in existence. I look forward to sharing with you the core of this story, and the expanded view within the scrolls to follow.

Chronicles of the Seventh Realm

River of Blood

Scroll 1

PROLOGUE

Trouble In Paradise

The mundane tasks of Eden's garden have grown trivial, as the animals, among other things, have all been named and now seek only council and comfort from Adam's blood. The family lay tightly packed under the Tree of Knowledge, and the children entertain themselves by pointing out shapes in the stars as they await peaceful slumber.

"The word is gal-ax-y…right, Mother?" the all-knowing feminine voice of a preteen asked; as her younger siblings blurted out words for each cluster they saw.

"Yes Deborah. Try not to be so critical, they're only pretending."

"Yes Mother, but…Father says its dangerous, and that words have power and…."

She was cut off by her father who said, "And they can leave lasting effects, Lilith, so Deborah is right—although it is difficult for them not to, they must try. We shall not have to re-record everything as it takes on a name given." He chuckled at the thought and continued. "Now go to sleep little ones; you will need your rest in order to grow."

The rest of the night passed without further discussion on the matter, but it wasn't long before Adam and Lilith were in disagreements again.

"Is this about what happened with Leo yesterday?" Lilith asked as she and Adam sat watching the children at play.

"Females are natural providers, Lilith; I do not see why there was even a need for discussion, or the resulting condition. I would have preferred an opportunity to weigh in before judgment was passed."

"Adam, you can not be in a hundred places at once, and I handled it. Those cubs are fully capable of providing for themselves. It isn't that much to ask of them to walk a few feet and reach for that which they desire. Sariah was trying to rest after a long day with the new cubs. I do not think an adolescent adding to that weariness by refusing to feed himself is appropriate, considering the circumstances."

"You decreed that all adolescents are to be removed from their parents' care."

"Adolescent males, dear," she interrupted, "and I do not think Leo was at all ungrateful for the provision. He has been concerned for a long time now that they spend too much time under the females, and your workload is vast enough."

Lilith was quiet then, as she noticed a few of the children paying attention to their discussion rather than playing in the garden, and thought it best to lower her voice. Adam did the same.

*

Laughter and joy filled the air as children played in the garden. A young boy of nine sat off to the side listening to his parents squabble in hushed tones.

"Look there, Lilith," his father said, pointing to a pair of dragonflies on the branch of a tree coupling. "Or there," he added, pointing off in the distance at a pair of zebras engaged in likewise activity. "He created all of us, yet they submit. Why do you find it such a daunting task to do the same?"

She looked down and pulled one of the toddlers at her feet into her bosom and looked at him. "Because he gave us domain over all, Adam…equally, and I say the submission should be shared. We don't…"

The boy stopped listening. He didn't know what the bid deal was, he only knew that whenever they argued, mother was unhappy. Pulling a few twigs off the ground, he started building stick figures. After several moments, he noted that the conversation must have been over, because his mother stormed away.

"I wouldn't ask her right now, Benjamin; give her a bit to calm down." Benjamin diverted his attention briefly to see who was speaking and sighed. He dropped the twigs he held in hand, and stood looking in the direction of his father.

"I don't know Tzofiya, the seasons are changing." He looked toward the direction his mother walked and continued shaking his head. "I'm not sure how long the window will be ope—"

His words were cut off and they both ducked low to the ground, covering their ears from the loud booming echo of his mother's voice as it rang throughout the garden. She'd said the forbidden word…she'd called out His name…the name of the creator…it was never to be said aloud. Benjamin found himself in tears as he instantly felt the loss of her presence. He held his ears tighter as he then heard the screams of his brothers and sisters. "Father," he cried, "what have you done?"

As the minutes turned into hours, and the hours turned into days, Benjamin longed for his mother. He's seen the creator speak to his father and waited patiently to know the news, but nothing could have prepared him for what he heard. Adam sat under the Tree of Knowledge and explained.

"I'm afraid your mother has refused to return. Others have been sent to speak with her, but it has been five days and her presence is greatly missed. I will not tell you that she will never return; however, as it is her decision to remain absent, it is my duty to inform you that it is a possibility she will not choose to return to us."

Groans, gasps, and cries filled the air as children of all ages complained. Everyone loved and missed their mother, but Benjamin held strong. He looked at Tzofiya, refusing to believe his mother would just abandon them. *This is Father's fault*, he decided and reached out for Tzofiya's comforting hand. The children sobbed for what seemed like an eternity alongside their father's hip. He too could not bear the loss after another day, and began sobbing as well. Not long after, everyone fell into a deep sleep.

Benjamin felt a gentle tug on his hand as Tzofiya's movements woke him, and he sat up looking around. At first he wasn't sure he was awake because the scene around him looked more like a dream than any reality he'd ever known. There were beings all around them—sort of human like Benjamin noted, almost exactly like his family…but they were different. They were all…glowing. *They're angels*, Benjamin said to himself, remembering the term his father used once.

"Hundreds of them," he said aloud. They were all pulling on his brothers and sisters. Tzofiya's gasp redirected his attention: she was looking up at the angel who carried her and tears began to fall down her cheeks. Benjamin frowned as he noticed the tears, and she sighed deeply. She then spoke as loud as her voice would carry.

"Benjamin. Run! They do not intend to take us all."

Benjamin blinked as he watched the scene in front of him. He didn't understand; his father was being tugged on, yelled at, and kicked by his children, but still he would not wake. He heard Tzofiya's voice ring in his ears as if she was right next to him "Run!" she'd yelled at him. Benjamin turned his head and a huge snarling beast, bigger that a horse, was headed right for him.

He then heard the screams of his brothers and sisters as those left behind were ripped to shreds by the beast that pursued him now.

"What's going on?" he asked no one as he ran toward the edge of the garden. Benjamin could hear the beast getting closer with every step. This situation was surreal; he wasn't sure if it was reality or a dream. Regardless, he was afraid.

"Up!" he heard his sister say. "You must climb up."

Without a moment to lose, he jumped at the first tree he saw and almost ran straight up, mere seconds before the beast lunged for his legs. It hit the base of the tree, and whimpered, then turned to chase down another one of his unlucky siblings.

At his example, others began to climb on whatever the beast could not. Benjamin noticed through the carnage that his father hadn't been touched. It was like he had an invisible protective ring around him or something, but it did nothing to help the children that crawled onto him for safety. The beast pulled on them all and hurriedly moved away from him.

Benjamin cried as he looked on, knowing there was nothing he could do for his siblings.

Morning came, and the angels were all gone, the beast ran off. Benjamin's face was red, his head hurt, and his throat ached. He tried to remember everything his sister told him throughout the night, but nothing was clear in that moment. The carnage was too great; he needed to get away from the scene. Several of his siblings had crawled out of their hiding places and attempted to wake their father again unsuccessfully.

Driven by fear, and the memory of his sister's words—*Run!*—Benjamin climbed out of the tree. He walked past so many bodies, trying to wrap his head around what happened, that he stopped counting. One of his elder brothers said, "There are at least a hundred dead here." If he had any tears left in his body, Benjamin would have wept for another seven days at the news. But he couldn't—all he could think about was getting the stench of blood out of his nose.

The day passed with almost no words spoken; everyone left alive helped in clearing the bodies to one side of the garden, and then collectively worked to make sure everyone was fed. The normal tasks for the garden seemed trivial and many of the animals were nowhere in sight. *They must have been spooked by the beast as well,* Benjamin thought.

Everyone gathered by the foot of their father waiting for him to wake.

Benjamin closed his eyes and tried to get some sleep. He could see his sister's face, but the words she mouthed were muted.

"What?!" he shouted, squinting at her image. She spoke again, but once again he could not hear her. He shook his head and shouted, "I can't hear you!" A second later, her image was replaced by the same snarling beast that chased after him the night before. His jaws were wide and he leaned in to devour Benjamin. He gasped sating up, and took several breaths. *Run!* Her voice echoed in his memory.

Benjamin wiped his eyes and looked around; his brows lowered as he noticed the sun starting to set. Many of his siblings began to voice their concerns, but Benjamin needed no convincing. Fear led him back into the tree, and by nightfall he was happy to have climbed higher than ever before because the snarling beasts were back. Benjamin shut his eyes tight and placed his palms over his ears, trying hard not to hear the screams of his siblings. Again, his father slept through the carnage and was passed over. Morning brought no relief and when the last beast was gone. Benjamin, along with many others, ran as far and as fast as they could from the Garden of Eden.

Chapter One

HIDDEN

Benjamin stopped a moment to catch his breath. He could hear the snarling beasts surrounding him, but he wasn't worried. In the past seventy years, he'd become somewhat of an expert at eluding them. What chased him now, however, he was not strong enough to fight alone. He may have been in the prime of his youth at 79, but Benjamin knew his limits, and he needed to focus. An archangel, even one he grew up with, would not stop to listen, even though it *was* an accident...*This time*, he thought, chuckling to himself as he ran.

Looking up, Benjamin smiled and jumped ten feet into the air, narrowly missing the fangs of one of the beasts that pursued him. He grabbed onto a tree branch and pulled himself up, swinging his body around it like an acrobat. He immediately began running along the branches of trees, confidence radiating through his features. *If I can just get to the pond, I will be safe,* he concluded.

Reaching the last tree, Benjamin paused and surveyed the area. The clearing in this part of the woods held a small pond, but most avoided it, instead staying on the path carved out by constant travelers. He smiled, looking down at his reflection: it was steady,

1

constant, unmoving, as if he'd looked into a mirror. No one else had joined him yet. He looked around…one leap and he'd be home, out of the realm of humans, and into the place between worlds where even the archangel wouldn't venture.

Identifying the packs whereabouts by their howls, Benjamin searched the trees. He looked along the ground, in shadowy places, and among the light. The full moon's glow shone overhead, and Benjamin was sure his movements would be noticed. *I'll have to time this just right,* he thought, leaning low on the branch.

As the sound of the approaching hounds grew nearer, Benjamin dove for his reflection and was violently tossed nearly three hundred yards away from his intended destination. He grunted as he rolled to his feet, and the hounds all charged at him. Extending his hands toward the beast, Benjamin knew he would be defenseless against the angel, but he had no choice. He released several balls of white light, which burned the beast and turned them all to ash. Exhausted, he fell to his knees, powerless to defend himself.

He was forced to his feet by the incredible strength of an archangel's grip around his neck. Benjamin tried to speak but only gurgles came out, so he laughed. "What's that?" the angel asked in a stern voice, then loosened his grip slightly. Benjamin could hear another pack of hounds approaching in the distance.

"Took you long enough," he repeated, a bit more audibly this time. The archangel released his hold on Benjamin and watched him fall to the ground.

He shook his head. "You cowardice rat!"

"And how am I like a rat, Constantine? Because I choose to live?" he continued without letting Constantine respond. "I am hunted, unlike you," he said, backing away from the angel and moving toward the pond. "And I will do whatever it takes to survive."

Constantine smiled crookedly. "Then I am pleased to inform you, brother, that your survival is no longer necessary." He reached for the sword at his hip and brought it high overhead.

Benjamin tried but could not move a muscle. Lightning struck the ground as Constantine brought the sword down. A clash of mettle rang in Benjamin's ears as another archangel shielded him. He looked the newcomer over with wide eyes mirrored by Constantine, who also looked enraged.

"Tzofiya, what is this?" he asked with lowered brows and wings agape. They both stood battle-ready and glowing slightly. They wore more gold than any being should ever wear at one time, and Benjamin found it difficult to stare directly at them. They were nothing like the angels he remembered seeing as a child, but they were angels nonetheless.

Her feminine voice rang out in his ears a song so beautiful it almost drowned out the hounds. He knew must be getting close.

"Please, Constantine; he didn't know what he was doing." She shook her head. "Banish him instead."

"And what, give him a chance to wreak havoc like Samael?" Constantine was pointing at Benjamin now. His sword was lowered slightly, but the expression he wore had Benjamin seeking the pond all the more urgently.

3

"His very existence is why we must fight to protect them Tzofiya, ending *his* life now will deny him any chance at making that task all the more difficult."

Waving his hand in the direction of the approaching hounds, Constantine tried to reiterate his point by reminding Tzofiya of their presence.

"Do you not hear that, sister? They hunt him every night. It's pure luck that he has eluded them this long, but his life is forfeited, sister. Let me pass." He brought his sword to the ready.

Tzofiya held steady and shook her head again. "No, Constantine, he deserves a chance. He has eluded them this long, and banishing him will keep him from harming them forever. He didn't know what he was doing, and thus should not be punished so harshly." Constantine growled, watching Benjamin inch toward the pond, and moved closer. Tzofiya mirrored his movements, backing up.

"Ignorance of the law does not free you from it, sister; that is how we gained our plot in this. Now please step aside."

Tzofiya shook her head once more, and Constantine sighed. He could hear the hounds as if they were at his back and turned to look in their direction. "So be it," he said.

"Then the hounds may have him." As he returned his attention to his sister, Benjamin stood and wrapped his arms around her frame. He leaped for the pond, and they both disappeared into the mirror and out of the realm of Adam.

The pair fell onto the ground and slid several feet. Tzofiya shoved Benjamin away from her and coughed as she waved her hand

4

about, trying to clear the dust cloud. She grunted and stood, spreading her winds wide. Sheathing her sword, Tzofiya began dusting herself off.

"It will take hours to get this grit out. Why would you do that?"

"I am sorry, sister, but there wasn't much of a choice," Benjamin lied with a smirk and rolled onto his feet. It would have been easier for him to take advantage of the archangel's distraction and jumped in alone, but he wouldn't pass up the chance to spend time with his sister. He hadn't seen her in so long, and she was the only one who would explain things to him. Hearing the tone in his voice, Tzofiya stopped what she was doing and looked at him with lowered brows, and her head tilted slightly. She opened her mouth to return an equally sarcastic remark and gasped, looking around.

It looked to her like they landed in a tunnel with crystal clear water floating all around them. Rainbows of color and the occasional change in scenery along the left and right walls were equally amazing. Tzafiya was visibly nervous.

"Benjamin, how did you find this place?"

"Come on," he commanded, taking her arm and pulling her along. "I'm not the only one who knows about this place." Tzofiya raised a brow, but said nothing further, only looked back once or twice as they moved along.

The pair of them walked along the tunnel until reaching a scene change in the walls that led to a vast mountainside full of lush greenery. "Through here," Benjamin said, pulling her along. When

5

they were fully within the realm, Tzofiya relaxed visibly and looked around.

"How did you find this place?" she asked again, reclaiming her arm.

"This way," he repeated, walking along as if she hadn't spoken.

There was a small opening at the base of a hillside almost hidden by the moss and foliage. Tzofiya lowered her brow and stopped. "Benjamin!" Sighing, Benjamin stopped and turned.

"Tzofiya, I will tell you what ever you want to know, but please, let me get you to safety first."

"Are you hunted here as well, Benjamin?"

He looked at her for a moment before responding. "Yes, we are hunted, daughter of Lilith." He shook his head. "But not by the hounds. Come on. There are many others willing to fulfill the quota of one hundred souls a day, and they do not care where they come from. The hounds that do make their way to the this realm are taken or killed."

As if to reiterate that point, six pair of dark red eyes appeared from out of the cave. Tzofiya watched as the hounds all came to rest on their hunches at Benjamin's feet. Raising a brow, Tzofiya looked on with interest.

The silent questions were deafening as Benjamin took the time to pet each of the beasts before continuing along the path that led deeper into the hillside. Tzofiya was amazed at the massive size of it—room after room they walked deeper into the heart of the mountain. Torchlight bounced off the walls along the path, and once they finally stopped, Tzofiya gasped. The huge hallowed out space was rich with foliage. A small stream of water ran through it, and the moonlight crept in through natural openings of the rocks in one place or another.

Chapter Two

BANISHED

Benjamin led Tzofiya to a small camp, complete with a fire, driftwood to sit on, and a lush bed of living leaves and flowers that reminded her of the garden they'd once called home. *How wonderful for him to have found such a lovely place in the mist of such chaos,* she thought, *and in the realm of knowledge no doubt.* Tzofiya smiled, watching as he disappeared behind one of the walls. Chuckling, she took a seat by the fire. *This will do perfectly.* He *will be safe here, and with his bodyguards,* she thought with a chuckle, *he can live out his days in peace.*

"Are you hungry?" Benjamin asked, interrupting her inner monologue. He'd returned with a huge leaf full of fruits and vegetables. He sat down next to her and grinned ear to ear. There was corn, carrots, apples, tomatoes, pears, bananas, and several other varieties of fruits. Tzofiya smiled and reached for an apple.

"Benjamin, how did you find this place? I mean the pathway, it isn't common knowledge."

Benjamin chuckled and picked up a tomato. "The last thing you said to me in the garden that night was 'run.'" He took a bite of the tomato, and smiled. Tzofiya couldn't help but chuckle at the juices that escaped down his chin.

"So I did...I ran right into this. It wasn't as vast as it is now." He said with a shrug and took another bite of the tomato; then moaned in satisfaction, closing his eyes and adding to the juices on his chin. Tzofiya rolled her eyes and took a bite of the apple.

"I wasn't followed," he continued once done with the tomato. He wiped the juices from his chin with a stroke of his palm, and Tzofiya took another bite.

"I stayed there all night, just watching, waiting, sure the hounds would pick up my scent." He shook his head. "But they never did. It was a solid week before I even started to feel hungry enough to venture out. I'd accepted your explanation by then, and was joined by several others who stayed only a brief while before moving on." He picked up a stick of celery. Tzofiya worked her way slowly through the apple, staring intently at the fire.

"It was hard at first, knowing that the lot of us would be hunted and killed simply because of our parentage." He took another bite and chewed it down before continuing.

"A hundred..." he said, contemplating a moment.

"I should never have told you that," Tzofiya added suddenly. Benjamin continued as if she hadn't spoken.

"But it was Mother's choice; we simply had to live with it. Or die trying." He chuckled dryly. "So I began a pattern: I would hop in and out of realms during the day, and stay in the...*pathway?*" he asked, looking at her with a raised brow, "by night. It wasn't long before I found out why father didn't wake up. He wasn't meant to remember us. Any of us." He returned his attention to the fire. "And his new mate quickly began replacing us. She submitted to his desires in ways Mother never would." Benjamin took another bite of the celery stick, and threw the rest into the fire.

"He completely forgot about us. Many were angered, and only made more so when they understood the decree that, because mother would not return, we would be hunted nightly. Those of us who survived grew stronger by the day, and more desperate. Some transformations have occurred, and those children of Lilith's not fathered by Adam sought revenge on us for their fate. They began to hunt us in addition to Eve's children. They hunt us still, sister, but many are killed in the process." He chuckled with a little more enthusiasm this time.

"It was all for naught, you know…. Seems Eve was worse than Mother, getting them all kicked out of the garden. At least mother left on her own accord." He sighed. "We live by day and exist only by night, Tzofiya, so forgive me for taking the opportunity presented when that daughter of Eve died in my arms."

Tzofiya stiffened hearing the last part and looked at him. "That is no excuse, Benjamin; ignorance of the law does not make you immune to its justice."

"Justice?!" he shouted, standing and swinging his arms about. "I am hunted because I exist." He came closer to her and pointed. "As you are, sister." He shook his head. "Don't look at me like that, and don't assume that your wings will save you from the night. For there are creatures we called siblings once who would surely take to the sky at a chance to cut you down if only to save its own life." He sat back down and stared at the fire with a humph.

10

Tzofiya moved closer to him and placed a hand on his shoulder.

"Did taking that woman's life-force shield you, Benjamin?"

"It did more than that, Tzofiya; for three days I was shielded from them. Those who hunted me met with abilities I'd only discovered defending myself from them." He released a small ball of yellow light into the fire, causing it to roar and hiss as it grew several feet before dying back down.

"I understand how it works now." He shook her hand off. "I will not be defenseless again."

Tzofiya replaced her hand. "What you've done, Benjamin, has turned the tables on the fight. How long do you think it will be before others see how weak they are? Or even try to do what you've done to end their suffering as you have yours, even if only for a brief moment?"

"Am I to pity them for that weakness, sister?" he asked placing a hand on hers and turning to face her. She attempted to pull away, but stopped in her efforts as he held on. "They may be Father's children, but they're weak and undeserving of the status they hold."

"Benjamin, I can not protect you from every archangel. If you go after another of Eve's children, you *will* be killed," she said, looking him in the eyes, trying to be sure he understood her warning. She blinked and lowered her brows. *Oh,* she said internally, trying to back away from him gently. She was surprised to feel a new kind of love for him now. A desire deep within herself she'd never allowed to surface, only telling herself that she protected him because she

11

cared for his life…. But now, staring into his eyes and knowing the comfort of his presence, she wanted only to be in his arms. She contemplated the reality of her emotions in that instant.

He was her brother, yes, misguided and lost, yes, but so was many of her other siblings. As children of Adam, her brothers and sisters were the only other people in the world. She spared a thought for Constantine. He was kind to her most days but like many others, he was more interested in forgetting the past than she would ever allow herself to. Benjamin knew her; he was her favorite, someone she could trust and confide in, and now maybe their relationship could reach a new level.

Benjamin must have been thinking along the same lines because he suddenly pulled her closer to him and crushed her lips with a kiss that left her wanting more. She moaned slightly, tilting her head and parting her lips as her hands hungrily moved about him. She braided her fingers in his hair and pulled herself closer to him. Benjamin growled as he held her, moving his hands along the small of her back, being careful of her wings. He pulled her closer. His hands moved along her hips, kneading at every part of her he could touch, and he paused in their embrace when he felt the sword at her hip. Tzofiya chuckled and stood, first removing her belt, then disrobing completely, she watched as he looked her over with wide eyes. Chuckling, she cleared her throat.

Benjamin stood there a moment looking her over, shocked at the turn of events. He couldn't help it; she was everything to him, and he'd wanted her from the moment he discovered what his parts were for. He quickly disrobed the simple cloak he'd tossed around himself, and the loincloth that covered his penis, and moved closer. She wanted him to, it seemed, and he would not let her go on wanting. He would take her, and if he died before the sun came up, this moment would make his entire existence worth living.

Benjamin moved closer to her, scooping her up into his arms and kissing her fiercely. He was startled for a brief moment when Tzofiya's wings opened suddenly, but not enough to break his hold on her. They were against the wall in the flash, his hands moving hungrily about her. He caressed and kissed every inch of her, taking special care not to damage her wings.

He didn't remember at what point they made it to the soft foliage, but there Benjamin moved with a bit more control— kneading rather than groping her breast, caressing her folds gently, kissing her along her curves. Tzofiya's moans of pleasure intensified as Benjamin licked along her inner thighs. Spreading her legs, he immersed himself in the nectar of her being.

When her rhythmic breathing paused, and her moans became screams that shook the very walls of the hillside, Benjamin unfolded himself from between her legs and prepared to enter her, but was surprised to find her suddenly on top of him, moaning just as loudly as her mouth engulfed his shaft. Benjamin grunted, leaning his head back, and curled his toes as he felt her warm moist tongue around the tip of his shaft. She ran her nails up the inside of his legs and gently tugged on his testicles.

Tzofiya kneaded them with one hand, and gripped the base of his shaft with the other. She twisted her head gently as she moved it up and down his member. Deep moans escaped her, vibrating

13

throughout his pelvic area. Pausing, Tzofiya pulled up on his shaft and made sure to roll her tongue around the very tip of his penis. She moaned in satisfaction as she felt herself release and paused a moment, closing her eyes.

Grunting, Benjamin reached down and placed a hand on her head, his toes curling more with every move she made. After a few moments, he could not take it anymore; he had to be inside her. Pulling her to his lips, he kissed her and rolled on top. Lifting her legs effortlessly, he inserted his penis into her warm wetness, moaning as a shiver ran up his spine. Thrusting forward, he explored the inner chambers of her being over and over again. As the night wore on, he filled her with every inch of him while trying different angles for them to explore each other.

By the time climax came, Benjamin was engulfed in her light; he didn't pull on her energy. He bathed in it, became engulfed by the good that was Tzofiya. He opened himself to her and moaned as he felt her reach for him. Unable to hold back, Benjamin released his seed deep inside her folds, and the entire hillside lit up with a golden hew that shown brightly in the night.

Benjamin wrapped his arms around Tzofyia and closed his eyes. Sleep took him soon after and he could hear her voice deep in his consciousness. He couldn't make out what she said, but he didn't have to. She was right there in his arms. She could tell him in the morning. Releasing the effort to understand her words, Benjamin drifted into a world of spinning color.

Chapter Three

TRAVELER

Benjamin sat up among the foliage and groaned. His head hurt and he felt like he could sleep another three days. Wiping the sweat from his brow, he pulled himself away from the foliage and leaned down to wash his face in the flowing creak. His sister's words rang in his ears, and he took a moment to search for her. Closing his eyes, he pulled on her light…nothing, so he gave up and continued on. It had been well over a thousand years now, but he remembered her words as if she'd jut spoken them.

"Light of my heart," she had said, masking the tears that threatened to take her words, "I banish you to a place where you can not touch another child of Eve. I banish you Benjamin, son of Lilith…." She paused and took a breath. "…To the realm of knowledge, where you can live out your days in peace. I banish you, my love, and I wish you only joy."

By morning she'd disappeared, and he'd tried for weeks to find her and a way to get out of this realm, but was unsuccessful. Tzofiya hadn't spoken directly to his mind since then, and Benjamin was often frustrated, but kept his attention on the constant battle at hand: staying alive. He petted the head of the beast closest to the hillside entrance, and looked out over the valley.

"I do not believe any of you will need feeding today, with all the ruckus I heard last night, there must have been three different packs you took down." The beast purred a deep rumble of satisfaction at the touch and leaned in a bit closer to him. Benjamin chuckled and petted him on the back. The beast laid his huge head on his paws and closed his eyes.

Benjamin squinted his eyes as he investigated the tree line. His eyes settled on a shadowy space for a moment, and he lowered his brows, flaring his nostrils as he tried to catch the scent of the intruder's light. The hound perked up its ears and lifted its head. Benjamin touched him reassuringly and said, "No, you've all done enough, I will take this one. Rest, you will be needed tonight." The beast dropped its head but kept his ears perked.

"Oh," Benjamin said as he picked up the scent of the intruder's light. He'd pulled on its energy and hit a brick wall. Smiling, Benjamin ran in the directions of the newcomer and was pleasantly satisfied to see him flee. "Not anymore," he said aloud. "If you hunt me, you pay the price." He increased his pace now, wishing to end the chase before it really began, but was foiled as the track suddenly went cold.

Benjamin stopped and flared his nostrils again, reaching, pulling, tugging on the creature's light, but he only got glimpses of where it was. Smiling, he ran for the direction he last sensed his light. It was a difficult task to keep up because the creature seemed to move sporadically. It was almost as of he was in several places at once.

"How is he doing that?" Benjamin asked, no one, lowering his brows. He was becoming winded, so he stopped and scanned for the creature's light again as he recovered his breath and gasped at what he felt.

There was an endless pool of energy here. "So bright," he said aloud. The rainbow of colors he felt swarming about energized him. He pulled on the endless pool and hit a wall. The force of its impact pushed Benjamin back several yards and he opened his eyes. He was confused. Searching the tree line, he saw hundreds of individuals moving about somewhat mundanely. Many of them were idly completing tasks: climbing trees, chopping down tree branches, picking up sticks and placing them about, walking from one tree to another and back. Benjamin did not understand any of it, but he was on a mission. He searched again for his intruder, and felt the creature's energy in the heart of the pool. He tried again to pull on it, and was knocked back with a bit more force this time.

"Who are you, seeker?" he asked aloud in a booming voice that was sure to carry into the pool of souls. "Why not come and take that which you seek? I am here. Come to me," he said with arms wide.

Without word or warning, the biggest snake he'd ever seen suddenly blocked his path. Benjamin searched for a way around the snake, but was stunned to stillness when it spoke to him, for the last time he'd heard an animal speak, he was in the Garden of Eden.

"Whatever you seek here, son of Lilith, you may not have these souls, for they do not belong to you. I must insist you continue on your way."

"And who might you be, creature of knowledge?"

"That too is none of your concern, but it if will help you along, I will be more than happy to oblige. I am Zelma, guardian of this pool, and you do not have permission to access it. Leave now, son of Lilith, and return to your lands or I will have no choice but to defend the souls you seek to claim."

Benjamin lowered his brows. "I do not seek to claim anything."

"Do not treat me as a simpleton," Zelma interrupted sternly. "I have felt your pull on my charges, and I will ask you only once to never do that again."

"I seek…" Benjamin continued as if she hadn't just threatened him, "only the traveler who sought to slay me." He gestured toward the souls. "He ran into your…." Benjamin stopped talking a moment and looked behind the snake into the wooded area, then said, "Pool?"

Zelma turned her head slightly, scanning the trees. Benjamin took the opportunity to seek out the intruder's light. It was faint, masked by the vast energy pool surrounding him. Zelma turned more of her coiled body toward the woods, searching it again, more intently this time.

Suddenly the light was gone and Benjamin was puzzled. Zelma turned to him with a look of uncertainty about her features, but only for a moment. "I do not see anyone here that does not belong, son of Lilith. Now go, and do not return."

Benjamin nodded and asked again, puzzled by the intruder's actions, and sure he himself would not have alerted the snake to his presence had he not reached for the energy pool: "What is this place?"

"A center of knowledge," Zelma replied and took off into the trees toward the direction Benjamin knew the intruder's light was centered just moments ago. Sure his chance at revenge was over for the moment, Benjamin settled for scanning the wooded area with his eyes, and climbed a nearby tree.

*

Sylvia panted as she ran, working hard to open each gateway and keep herself shielded. If she could just get to the pathway, it would be easier for her to open a gateway home. Malikye warned her of creatures like this, but she never thought she'd come up against one—at least not one she couldn't defeat…well…she hadn't so far. Sylvia panted and released her shield, then pulled deep within herself and opened a gateway at the edge of the knowledge realm.

Sprinting through it, Sylvia dove for the souls of the realm and knew she had precious little time. She could not hold a shield here, or she'd risk exposure to the guardian, so she ran as fast as she could to the pathway. With so many souls cloaking her light, she was almost positive the creature that sought her now would be lost. She dashed through trees and climbed over branches, ducking and spinning when necessary, taking care not to touch anyone she came across. That would surely alert the guardian.

Sylvia reached the pathway faster than she anticipated and was elated to see it clear. Normally it would take a bit of distracting the souls to move the guardian, but today she was gone. Things could not have been better if she'd planned them herself. She approached with caution, watching the narrow space that held the shimmering path. She opened herself up only when she reached the pathway, and created a gateway home.

Darting through, she crashed into her wardrobe and amidst the realm of Adam's blood. Panting, Sylvia vowed internally to never cross paths with such a creature again. She would continue hunting the sons and daughters of Lilith, but never again in the seventh realm. Her son's life was important to her, but she had to live long enough to keep him safe from the hounds.

Chapter Four

BOUNDARIES

Benjamin leaned back onto a tree at the top a hillside overlooking the valley below. He stretched out his legs and crossed them at the ankles. Slicing into an apple, he offered part of it to one of the beast at his feet. The creature let out a deep rumbling purr and put its head down. "No?" Benjamin shrugged and popped the slice into his mouth.

Another three slices of the apple found its core, and Benjamin chewed contently as he looked out into the vas pool of souls gathered in this place. He'd come to understand these fields a little better. There were seven of them in total, and though he could not leave this realm, he'd heard of many others with pools of their own, some big enough to dwarf the seventh realm a hundred times over. The pool of souls he stared into was filled with individuals idly working toward enlightenment through mundane tasks.

Many were the sons and daughters of Eve. One of the souls clapped as she finished building a campfire, and disappeared. Another walked into a wall of trees, backed up, and started slowly walking around them in circles. Another ran from tree to tree then back again; he repeated this cycle before working its way up the tree. *How convenient,* Benjamin thought, and tossed the core aside.

Although Benjamin learned more and more about the souls on a daily basis, his interest was never focused on why they were here, but instead how best to gain access to their light. *If one dying daughter of Eve could be so powerful, I can only imagine what a single pool of this size will do.* Sitting up straighter, Benjamin noticed a clumsy trespasser who'd unintentionally run into several moving souls within the field, and drew the guardian's attention. He quirked a brow. "That's never a good idea," he said aloud.

Benjamin watched as the massive bird swooped down and grabbed the intruder. Her huge claws curled around him with ease, threatening his very existence should he move a muscle. The man cowered in her hands begging once he heard her speak.

"Why have you come to this garden, riffraff? There is nothing for you here." She tossed the man on the ground and squawked at him, her chest puffed out.

He rolled several feet before coming to a stop. When he did, the man quickly rolled onto his belly and begged to be forgiven.

"Oh please, great one, I came upon your garden by accident."

"Accident!" the bird repeated angrily. "One doesn't enter my garden by accident, riffraff. Out with it. What are you doing here?"

"I am sorry, great one," he apologized again, placing his head to the ground as he spoke. "I was being chased and thought to hide inside; I meant no harm. Please…."

22

Benjamin stopped listening then, and focused his attention on three individuals within the mass of bodies that seemed to be moving a bit differently than the rest.

"What's this?" he asked no one. There was a woman strangely dressed from head to toe in garb to match the surrounding forest. The two males with her were dressed in camouflage as well. Benjamin looked on with renewed interest, as the three seemed to be herding one of the souls away from its intended path. They didn't touch it, but forcefully placed themselves in its path, making the soul move where they wanted him.

"Interesting," Benjamin said, and turned his attention back to the guardian who was now turning her attention back toward the souls. She stopped hearing a sheath sword come free.

"I presume your pursuers have returned, riffraff?" she asked with interest. When the man grinned evilly and advanced toward her, she turned her body to face him.

Benjamin shook his head. "Wrong answer," he said, returning his attention to the small herding party. They'd managed to get the soul outside the protected forest, but were having trouble now moving him forward. The man stumbled blindly as he blinked, trying to focus.

The bird seemed mildly irritated by the intruder's advances as the herding party struggled with the soul. The man leaped forward, confident in his attempt at cutting down the bird who squawked angrily, and opened her huge wings, lifting slightly off the ground as she brought her claws forward to address him. The intruder ducked and dodged the claws as he tried to find an opening,

23

rolling onto the ground whenever she got close enough to swipe at him. The man rolled as the tip of her claw caught him across the arm, leaving his skin in searing pain. It sizzled, and the man grunted as he wavered on his feet.

His discomfort did not go unnoticed, and the herding party paused in their efforts and looked toward his direction a bit panicky. The woman took a small jar from her belt and pulled a knife from her sleeve. She sliced open the throat of the bewildered spirit and held the jar close to the incision. Benjamin raised a brow as a river of gray smoke glistened and poured into the bottle.

Sighing, Benjamin stood and reached deeply within himself. Combining the elemental energies around him and adding a few touches of his own, as he'd come to discover them through collecting the souls of his pursuers, he grunted and tossed up a shield. He was sure to include as many of the hounds as he could, but would not push himself. The light of those who chased after him was effective enough to boost his existence, but not nearly as powerful as the child of Eve. Moreover, he may have figured out his intruder's tricks for the most part, but he was still amateurish when it came to using them.

The bird squawked, feeling the loss of her charge, and rounded on the herding party, tossing the man aside with her giant wings. He rolled several feet before coming to a stop, unconscious. She made her way back to the others as they released the soul and he fell to the ground. The woman quickly corked the bottle and slipped it into her pocket, yelling for the others to fall back.

The bird made her way between the remaining souls and the herders. She lowered her head, sniffing at them intently. Without a word, she paused, opened her wings, and inhaled deeply. Her chest full of air, she let out a squawking roar so deafening that the herders were knocked to the ground, screeching in pain as they held their ears. The ground rumbled and the nearby trees were uprooted and tossed roughly a thousand yards. Blood ran from the herder's eyes, ears, nose, and mouth. After a moment, they were still, then vanished.

Benjamin was impressed with himself. This was the first time his shield held up to an attack from a guardian. His ears rang, and he lost three hounds in the process, but he was alive…and well. All ten fingers, and all ten toes—he laughed and looked down into the valley, watching the animal. The guardian walked over to the soul and gently picked him up. She spread her wings wide and took to the sky.

The huge bird disappeared shortly thereafter, and Benjamin dropped his shield. He stood and leisurely walked down to where the confrontation had taken place and looked around. Coming upon the misty bottle, Benjamin smiled, bent to pick it up, and headed as far away from the tempting pool of souls as he possibly could. *Now is not the time…but soon*, he told himself.

Benjamin's evening progressed rather uneventfully. He set the hounds to their post and retreated into his cave. Deep within, he came upon a room only used now for the development of his gifts. The walls were charred a dark grayish black, and only a stone slab lay in the middle of the room. It was often the target of his exercise. It

25

began as a large piece of stone simply protruding out of the floor, but was now reduced to a table. He chuckled, looking it over, and wondered briefly what he would use when it was gone. Moving closer to the slab, he placed the bottle directly in its center and stepped back, considering how to move forward.

Pacing the room, Benjamin recalled what he currently knew. To date, he'd discovered that a variety of different light energies could be expelled from him: white, yellow, blue, and green. Some were made more powerful with the aid of energy from natural resources such as plants, stones, water, and many others. It was more beneficial to him, however, to use the remains of his victims—those who had sought to cause him harm. Man or beast, it made little difference to him, but the energy often altered and extended from him in strange ways. It drained him when his host was dead, and thus far working on a live willing subject was proving to be difficult.

Benjamin chuckled at the thought and continued his internal deliberation. He needed his hounds because others would continuously hunt him. Shrugging, he tapped his chin, pausing in his pacing a moment. *If Samael wants to keep sending the beast, I'll simply keep taking them,* he concluded. He picked up the bottle and consumed its contents.

Benjamin gripped his throat and coughed, dropping the bottle onto the stone floor. He fell to his knees, heaving as he tried to regain his breath. He extended a hand toward the table but just missed the edge and fell to the floor unconscious....

Benjamin suddenly found himself violently pulled through a tunnel of bright white light. Every so often he was slammed into a barrier so hard that his sleeping body shuddered on the cave floor. He was abruptly pulled to a stop where he was forced to close his eyes momentarily in order to adjust to the bright light on the other side. He blinked several times, adjusting to his surroundings.

Benjamin had been staring into the bright end of a tiny flashlight. "Just follow the light, Mr. Frost," Benjamin heard a feminine voice order. He tried to turn his head. He felt the woman place her soft hand upon his brow. Benjamin recoiled from the contact.

"Oh, no, no, Mr. Frost, please hold still. You took a nasty spill there…." She smiled and backed up a bit, turning the flashlight off. "You have a small bump on your head, but it will go away with time. I removed your…"

"Daughter of Eve," Benjamin interrupted her, looking around. He was lying on the sidewalk of a parking structure. An ambulance was backing up toward him and the small crowd of onlookers and medical responders surrounded him.

"Pardon?" the woman asked with lowered brows. The ambulance stopped and the doors opened. Two others stepped out.

"You…" Benjamin repeated again, pointing at her for emphasis, then looked around, taking in more of his surroundings. "You are a daughter of Eve."

The woman shook her head. "No my mother's name was Doris…"

"And this is the realm of Adam," Benjamin interrupted again, getting to his feet.

27

The woman shared a look of alarm with the paramedics and reached a hand out for Benjamin. "Mr. Frost, are you alright?" she asked, placing a hand on his arm. Benjamin backed away from her with lowered brows. "My condition is none of your concern daughter of…." Abruptly he cut off, hearing a strange voice in his head: *What are you doing in here?* Benjamin paused. "You're still here?" He paused, then added, "I'd hoped you were dead." He sighed. "This will make things more difficult."

"Mr. Frost, please calm down, who are you talking to?"

Benjamin ignored her and continued. "I hadn't planned on entertaining your consciousness, but I gather it will suffice. There are several things I must attend to first. Where is the…?" Benjamin grunted as he was pulled back suddenly and tossed onto a stretcher. Two large males held him down and he growled, trying to pull himself up. "Let go of me." *This is impossible,* Benjamin concluded, and reached for Frost's light.

At the same time, the woman injected a sedative into his arm saying, "There you go Mr. Frost, we'll have you feeling better in no time; don't worry."

Benjamin was violently tossed back into his own body. Immediately, he pulled on the man's energy. He heard a screeching howl within his own mind so loudly that he ears rang and his eyes watered. He paused a moment to let his sound tolerance return before speaking to the soul.

"Frost, is it? Can you explain to me what happened to you?" Benjamin could feel his agitation, his confusion, and his fear as if it was his very own. He took several calming breaths. *I have come too far to quit now,* he reasoned, and listened closely for the soul's explanation.

Speaking in short burst as if he'd been physically exhausted, Frost began: "I'm...yes, my name is...is Jeffery Frost...please, I...I was just going to do some light shopping at the mall and, ...and when I went through the door...I ended up in here."

"Where are you?"

"It's...some kind of a cage."

Benjamin's brows lowered. "Hmm."

"Then...well, you came...and...now, there is pain...please, whoever you are, can you stop the pain and let me out of here?"

Pain... Benjamin focused now. He was glowing outwardly, and noticed the howling of approaching hounds in the distance. He decreased his pull on the soul's light gently, tugging at it. If he lost the connection now, he might not have enough light to get past the barrier, which held him here.

"I cannot release you just yet, son of Eve, but perhaps in time. Now, try and relax."

I have to do this properly. The soul's not dying this time around, and I didn't put him in that cage. If done properly, Jeffery should survive the experiment. Benjamin took a deep breath and kept his pull on Jeffery's light as if it were a single flame atop a candle he needed to keep burning even as the wind blew all around. He felt it within himself as a numbing tingle of his senses.

Benjamin slowed his breathing, working to decrease his heart rate while focusing in on a tiny flame. "Jeffery Frost," he said aloud, and was pulled into Jeffery's memories. He saw him being born, was pulled through his early life as if time itself moved him forward. He watched as Jeffery struggled through high school in a blur, and again as he entered the workforce. Jeffery's smarts moved him forward in his career in spite of the struggles he'd experienced in high school.

Benjamin frowned as he watched the moving scenes of Jeffery's life, and all his first time experiences. As Benjamin came to Jeffery's current circumstance, Jeffery's mind brought him to an abrupt stop. Benjamin watched as Jeffery was cared for while sitting in a wheel chair overlooking a vast garden. A woman came nearer to Jeffery and spoke to him. She looked him in the eyes, but he was more distant now than he'd been moments before when Benjamin spoke to his mind. Sighing, he released his tug on Jeffery's light, and was pleasantly surprised to find that his connection to him remained.

Chapter Five

SENTENCED

Tzofiya sat twirling her thumbs, wearing an expression of annoyed frustration. She couldn't understand why she needed to explain things all over again. *He needed to be stopped, so I stopped him. Bound him away from the realm of Adam forever. He will never be able to touch another child of Eve. What's the point of the continued questions? ...My answer will not change no matter how many times I'm asked,* she reasoned as she sat, waiting to be called. She could hear Constantine's protest all the way out here. Rolling her eyes to his words, she looked around a moment then stood and walked over to the window.

The water broke the banks in a rush, and Tzofiya saw Benjamin's face in her mind's eye. The office building she now stood in disappeared, and she closed her eyes. Well over a thousand years had gone by, but she could still feel him touch her, hold her, and kiss her as if it were yesterday. Tzofiya let her mind wander. She smiled, thinking of his tender touch on her wings.... Her reverie was broken; she had to be called twice by the attending angel.

She blinked several times and looked at the woman a moment, then nodded. The angel was a fairly short woman. She

31

wore her hair pulled back in a tight bun. The green thong matched her dress perfectly, and Tzofiya smiled, thinking it was more form fitting than professionalism called for. *But I guess it's professional enough,* she noted, seeing the thin green belt that held it all together.

"Thank you," Tzofiya said, moving toward the direction she indicated. The angel smiled as she led the way past a smirking Constantine who sat watching Tzofiya accusingly as they passed. Behind a pair of French style doors, a woman and man sat waiting. There was no desk in this office. It was a round room with four chairs that sat around a large sunburst in the floor. The attendant smiled as Tzofiya made her way farther into the room, and pulled the doors shut behind her. She went back to her desk and Tzofiya looked intently at the pair who silently judged her.

No matter how many times she saw them, she was never comfortable around these angelic beings, and often wondered who they were, and where they came from. Rumors were ramped when the chosen were first brought here and given the choice to serve or be tossed back into the garden with their dying brothers and sisters. Many believed they were also children of the garden, but perhaps from another time.

The pair still radiated slightly, but wore a modern look of white-collar society. *As if they would ever be mistaken for human.* Tzofiya chuckled internally at the thought and sat down adjacent to the pair, who watched her every move. As she came to a rest, they began speaking in turn, one after the other and often finishing one another's sentences until they past judgment.

"Tzofiya, daughter of Lilith," the female began, "archangel and guardian to the children of light."

"You have been summoned here because you stand accuse of interfering with the sentencing of a lawbreaker," the man finished. "The decision you made to banish Benjamin, son of Lilith, prey to the hounds of the deep…"

"Has turned out to be much more harmful than any one could have realized at the time," the woman said.

"What has happened?" Tzofiya interrupted.

"You will let us finish, guardian," the male responded forcefully, then continued. "Because of your actions, humanity is at a far greater risk."

"It is unclear at the moment how far Benjamin has grown, and what he will accomplish, because we are shielded."

Shielded? she repeated internally, lowering her brows.

"But his recent actions have shed a new light on his existence." They paused in their speaking, and gestured to the sunburst on the floor, which began to glow.

Tzofiya saw Benjamin and her heart skipped a beat. She watched as he consumed the vial's contents, then was whisked across worlds and into the soul's consciousness. She saw everything he'd done, until the moment he was expelled back into his own body. She sank back in her chair and sighed audibly.

Understanding was clear then. Although he was not free to roam the realm of Adam physically, Benjamin had found a way to gain access to their precious light, and there was no telling what he was capable of now. Tzofiya sighed again and looked up at the pair.

33

A part of her was proud of him for surviving this long, and wanted to reach out, scoop him up in her arms, and never let him go. The other part of her wanted to strangle him for shedding light on himself again and putting her charges in harm's way.

"You are tasked with aiding the wise ones in their struggle to care for and protect the souls of the seventh realm," the male said while getting to his feet. He walked over to her and placed a thumb directly in the center of her forehead. A golden light ran through her. She glowed for a moment, then her wings were absorbed into her back, leaving a dark tattoo across her entire back in their stead. Tzofiya gasped and fell to the floor, exhausted.

"Watch over them," the woman said, "and keep those within the seventh realm at bay."

Tzofiya tried to protest, but was overcome with fatigue. Her eyelids drooped and sleep over took her. When next she woke, she was laying between two trees, in the middle of a foliage-rich pond.

*

Sylvia rocked slowly in the chair as she held her son close. His fever would pass, she knew; it was just a scratch after all. In the past five years since she'd lost her mate, she constantly worried whenever he fell ill. She frowned...a rusty nail wouldn't claim her son's life, she tried to convince herself. *Not if I have anything to say about it.* She reached over and grabbed a cloth that sat in a misty bowl and squeezed the water from it. The skills she learned from Malikye were incredibly effective, and although they did not stop the chase, they helped to cloak the part of her son that was Lilith. She placed the cloth along the boy's head and continued rocking in the chair. He shivered and moaned in his sleep, but otherwise stayed still.

Sylvia sighed after he settled back into a rhythmic sleep. The only worry she had now was the dwindling days he had left without the cloak. *Seven days' grace*, she thought. With the fever, there was no option left but to remove the protective cloak. She looked at the defensive words around the room and sighed. *I have to buy him more time. It will have to be an elder*, she concluded, and searched her memory for places she knew to find one.

*

Reuben groaned as he lay among the battered ground. Every part of him hurt. He'd watched as the massive bird murdered his siblings, helpless to defend them. Everything inside of him yearned to taste its blood, but his vengeance would have to wait. He would have his day, he vowed, *and a thousand more pets to replace the ones you took*. He was week and found it difficult to move among the rubble of trees, so he laid his battered body atop a fallen tree to rest. Chances were, the beast would not even notice him, and he could collect the bottle now without any further confrontation.

Reuben sighed and closed his eyes a moment. Movement among the rubble had him straining to see. He forced his eyes open and saw a man pick up his hard-earned bottle of essence and place it into his pocket. In his weakened state, Reuben could only watch. He burned the image of the thief's features into his mind, closed his eyes, and vowed to find him again once he regained his strength.

*

Benjamin grunted with the effort as he tossed energy ball after energy ball at the barrier along the pathway. He wanted off this prison, and could see that his efforts were affecting the shield, but he was growing week. He would run out of energy long before he could even prick the barrier. Benjamin briefly considered pulling on Jeffery's light and lifted the shield, protecting his mind from feeling the soul's discomfort, and immediately tossed it back up.

The only way to pull enough of his light to further effect the shield will leave him dead, and I an not quite ready for that, nor am I sure it will even be enough, he reasoned, tossing another energy ball at the all but invisible barrier. It flexed like a balloon momentarily, and then dissolved into nothing before withering away completely.

Benjamin inhaled deeply, wiped the sweat from his brow, and sat down a moment. "There has to be a way," he said to no one, and lowered his brows, studying the shield intently. A familiar feeling came over him. Someone burst through the shield and ran past him in a blur. He smiled, placing the familiar feeling. "Intruder," he murmured, then projected himself into the mind of the beast furthest from him.

The animal ran faster closing the distance, sniffing and searching out the familiar scent. Benjamin smiled and returned to his own body. He followed after them, swiftly fighting the desire to reach out for the intruder's light. "You won't get away from me this time, hunter," Benjamin said.

When he caught up to the beast, it was silently stalking the intruder from roughly 350 yards away. He'd climbed up a tree and was looking out over a vast open area, unaware of the danger lurking at his back. Benjamin smiled with eyes on his target, and reached for the intruder's light, gently tugging. A shield went up, and the figure jumped from the tree. Before he could take a step, however, Benjamin tossed an energy ball at him. "Stay!" he ordered with a grin.

The figure grunted and fell forward. Immediately, Benjamin pulled firmly on his light and ran up to him. Using his foot, Benjamin turned the now sleeping figure over, and lowered his brows. "Daughter of Eve," he said, surprised, as he released the woman's light. Benjamin looked at her a moment contemplating, then blinked and bent to secured her unconscious body to the back of a hound. When finished, he headed for his valley among the hills.

*

Sylvia opened her eyes and looked around. She reached up to place a hand on her pounding head, but couldn't move it. In fact, she couldn't move either of them. Panic overwhelmed her and she tried to stand. Grunting, she realized the problem—she was bound. Her hands were secured behind her back, and her legs were tied at the ankles. She sighed and tried to focus on her surroundings a little better. *Where am I?*

She'd been placed in a cave of some sort, and was a bit high up off the ground. *Looks like a table,* she thought. *Hmmm.* Lowering her brows, she noticed light creeping in from corners and slight breaches in the cave walls. She smiled seeing her backpack on the floor and turned herself over. A loud thud escaped her as she fell to the floor. Wasting no time, she began squirming and moving about from left to right, anchoring herself with the foot of the table. She smiled, maneuvering her bound hands around effortlessly, pulling them in front of herself.

Lifting her hands to her mouth, Sylvia began working at the binds around her wrist. She smiled to herself, feeling them coming free of the ropes, and worked faster. She tossed the ropes aside once free, then sat up. Leaning forward, Sylvia worked feverishly at the binds around her ankles. She chuckled when done, kicking them off, then turned over and crawled toward her bag. With one hand outstretched, Sylvia froze at the sound of a deep voice.

"You didn't really think I'd make it that easy, did you?" Immediately she tossed up her shield, and was flung half way across the room by the light emanating from the man's hand. The impact of her back hitting the table leg knocked the wind out of her, and her shield fell.

"Do not do that again, daughter of Eve." With a wave of his hand, the binds found their way around her wrist again, and the man walked closer to her.

Her eyes grew as she realized whom it was, and she scrambled for her things. Sylvia reached her bound hands out toward it and his boot secured them in place. He bent and held a finger out to her. He shook it, making a *tsk, tsk* sound. "You have some explaining to do first, daughter of Eve.

Sylvia sighed and panted heavily as she spoke. "My...name...is Sylvia Hernandez Elder. What is it you wish an explanation to?"

While she spoke, Benjamin lifted her bag and turned it over, pouring its contents onto the floor. Inside, she'd placed a few protection supplies and trapping tricks. There were oils, herbs, a few crystals; she even included the tiny bones of birds. Benjamin paid no attention to any of them, and bent down to grab her up by the binds. He effortlessly pulled her onto the table and lifted her black shirt. Sylvia's chest heaved as she breathed, realizing what he was referring to. She was frigid as he pulled her jeans down about two inches and pointed.

"Desire, body, mind, skill, motivation, valor, universe," Benjamin said as he made his way around the symbol drawn on her abdomen. For emphasis, she'd included a small drawing of the guardians that protect the fields around the hexagram. There was a snake, bird, panther, praying mantis, wolf, and dragon.

"This is how you make your way into and out of their fiends undetected," he accused. Sylvia's eyes lowered in suspicious surprise. "One does not exists in the realms of knowledge for as long as I have without picking a few things up," he said in response to her expression. "I don't care much for the reason you've come, hunter; show me how."

"Gateways?" she asked, even more surprised now.

"Gateways," Benjamin repeated more to himself as if he realized that he'd known of them all along and was now being reminded.

"Yes." He nodded. "Gateways," he said a bit louder this time. "Show me."

Releasing her hands, Benjamin cut through the binds and stood back, looking at her expectantly as he crossed his arms. Sylvia sat up and scratched her head, looking at him, puzzled, for a moment. At the dark look that replaced expectation, she began.

"I'm sorry…it's just, an elder taught me." She shrugged. "I am just a little taken aback that you don't know how." His growl had her tossing up her hands defensively and she quickly added, "But I don't mind showing you. Not at all." She took a deep breath and stood, looking at her things spread across the floor longingly. *I'll have to get more*, Sylvia thought to herself. *If he is crazy enough to trust me, I won't need my shield. I'll just open a gateway to my home, and the minute he steps through it, he's mine.*

The hint of a smile crossed her features and Benjamin raised a brow. Sylvia extended it, smiling brightly at Benjamin.

"Malikye told me you have to focus on where you want to go," she began.

"Malikye!" Benjamin exclaimed, watching her with an expression of suspense about his features. Her arms went high above her head a moment, and the symbol drawn on her midsection started to glow. Directly in front of her a hole erupted, spitting small burst of light into the air as it grew. When finished, it was roughly the length of Sylvia's body and as wide as a door. Without a second to lose, she bolted for it in a bit of a run, but fell to the floor screeching in pain, half her body sprawled at the bottom of the gateway in between both realms.

Benjamin ignored her attempt at escape and reached for her light, pulling firmly. "I told you it's not going to be that easy. Now why would Malikye show you this?"

"But...but I showed you...you said you didn't care about the rest. Let me go!" Her hands gripped ether side of her temples, and she cried out in pain.

With one hand Benjamin pulled her back and repeated the question. "Why would Malikye show you this?" He remembered his brother just two years his senior; he'd ran from the trees along with several others the moment the beast wandered off. He was smart—very smart—and certainly would not have simply shared this knowledge with a daughter of Eve. Benjamin looked at the gateway, waiting for Sylvia to recover, gently tugging on her light.

Benjamin could see the energies composing the light binding around the gateway; he could feel its pull on the surrounding's energies, and was confident he could do it himself. Sylvia groaned and panted as she spoke again.

"He...said I could learn...said we'd be safe. But he did not know the—"

"We..." Benjamin interrupted. As if in response to his question, a young boy came in to view. He was wearing pajamas and called out as she moved toward them.

"Mamma? Is that you?"

"Run, Filat!" Sylvia screamed at him. But it was too late; Benjamin had already reached out for the boy's light. Gently he tugged on the boy, who instantly fell to the ground unconscious. His mother begged his release; she crawled forward, trying to claw her way through the gateway.

The boy was different; his light was brighter, much brighter than his mother's somehow. It was almost as bright as…. Benjamin's eyes widened and he released the boy. He backed up slightly, letting go of the woman's light, who instantly crawled to her son's side, begging again for his release.

"That's Malikye's son?!"

"Yes," the woman replied, tears streaming down her cheeks.

"And the only reason I hunt. Please," she begged again, returning across the gateway on her knees, looking up at him. Benjamin looked down at her disgusted now, and backed away slightly.

Sylvia fell forward and stayed where she was begging again.

"Please, Elder, I will never hunt in this realm, again please I beg you to release him. I will be content to chase those of lesser realms and blood."

Benjamin ignored her pleadings and walked around her to the gateway. He stood mere inches away, and Sylvia turned her body so it was still submissive, but she could also keep an eye on her son.

Benjamin reached out and lightly tugged on both their lights, then tentatively reached a hand through the gateway. His hand burned as it crossed over the barrier. The skin darkened as smoke poured from his fingers. He grunted, pulling his hand back, and growled. Though he instantly felt relief, the damage stayed unchanged. Sylvia's eyes widened about two inches, and she lifted her head slightly.

42

"I am sorry if you can not cross over, Elder; I'm sure it's the wards I've placed. I would be happy to make another one."

Benjamin looked down, seeing her then. *It's possible, but at great cost,* he concluded, looking down at his hand again. He then realized the woman's words: *"Make another,"* she'd said, *so she's not restricted to this one place,* he reasoned. *Perfect.*

"The child will be fine, and there will be no more of this elder you seem so fond of calling me; you will address me henceforth as Master." He bent down and touched her head, projecting a combination of his own light energies into her. She gasped, feeling the cold run through her body, and fell over. Her breathing came in short pants as she looked at him, trying to pull herself up. She then looked at her son as he spoke.

"And he is to come to me when he reaches the age of fifteen years. Any descendent of yours is mine, and the rule applies to them also. Teach them well; they will need your skills to serve me. Now go, Mine; I will call on you when I need you again."

*

Sylvia felt ice run through her body as he touched her skin. She lost control of her limbs a moment and fell over onto the floor. She panted, listening to the elder speak. *Is he serious?! He can't even cross the gateway.* She watched her son's steady breathing and thought the elder was mad, but if it got her away from him with her son's life, she would play along. She noticed the pain that had gripped her before was gone, and looked up at him.

Clearing her throat, Sylvia asked, "Master...." She tried the words for show. "How do I protect him for another seven years if I am to do your bidding? It will be difficult to hunt."

Benjamin looked at her, seemingly calculating his options for a moment, and then called out. It sounded more like a grunt then a yell to Sylvia, and within seconds, beast after beast filled the small space. She gasped. *He's serious!* Her brows lowered as he spoke again.

"You are welcome to raise him here if you choose, Mine, but if you insist on staying where you are, take them and try not the get them all killed." Sylvia looked at the eyes and counted seven pair. She nodded absently to him.

"Yes, of course." The look he gave her had her shrinking back and she quickly added, "Master?" then scrambled through the gateway to her son's side. He was beginning to stir.

The beast filled in after her, and when she was sure they were not going to attack, she tried raising her shield once more. It fizzled and dissolved to nothing in her mind.

"That will no longer work on me, Mine; be sure and teach your offspring to obey as well or he will learn as you do the consequences of defiance."

"Yes, Master," she replied and closed the gateway. Sylvia looked at the beast, wondering how she was to care for them. "They will feed themselves," she heard the elder explain and gasped, wondering how he knew what she was thinking. She shook her head again as tears fell down her cheeks.

Chapter Six

REVENGE

Jeffery sighed as he paced the small confines of his cage. He was tired of being in here. Tired of feeling the constant pull on his mind. Tired of the confusing answers he always got that didn't explain the how or why of his current circumstance. He just wanted to be home, back in his own world. Benjamin, as he had come to know the name of the man who called himself his master, was not responsible for him being caged, but he often made matters worse by causing him constant headaches. He'd had so many of then now that he'd begun to think it strange to be without one. He sighed again and sat back down, thinking of the sun. There were only clouds here, and he was sure the cage was suspended somehow, so even if he did find a way to get out of it, he was sure he'd fall to his death.

"Well come on then," he heard a feminine voice beckon.

"Unless you *want* to stay in there, but I'm not telling him no. You can do that yourself." Jeffery blinked, unsure he could trust his ears. The only communication he had in all this time was through internal methods. First, it was Benjamin. Then an archangel who explained that nothing could be done to get him out at the moment.

45

There was a glowing female who didn't look much like any female he'd ever seen, who asked him a bunch of questions and then told him his light was misplaced. He shrugged, thinking of that response. She'd told him staying put was his best option…as if he had any clue what that meant. Jeffery blinked again, his eyes focusing on the woman who stood at the opening now. When she didn't move, and the voices in his head stayed quiet, he stood up and walked out of the cage.

*

Benjamin grunted, his arms shook, and the veins in his neck looked like they would pop out at any moment. He was glowing slightly and his grunts turned into a slow but climbing growl as he pulled on the light of all three charges. His difficulty came as he tried to keep his shield up and only tug at the boy's light. It was so tempting, and his to take. He panted and released the three of them, gasping with his palms on the almost invisible barrier. He was slightly orange in color now as he stood there mixing the light energy around within his being.

A crowd had gathered around Benjamin, and while many of them simply watched with growing amusement, some tried to attack when they thought him weak. Others ran through the barrier teasingly, offering more entertainment as they occasionally flew back when Benjamin actively tossed energy balls at it. He held so much blood energy inside of him now that every time he tossed a ball at the shield, it came out white and slightly misty. Benjamin heaved as he released another ball and inhaled deeply, plopping down onto a soft pillow someone brought over in gratitude for the entertainment.

Taking a cleansing breath, Benjamin gulped a few swallows of water from the sheepskin at his feet. He looked up at the sun and grunted; its intense heat seamed to pull at his energy as well. Sighing, he took a few more breaths and wiped the sweat from his brow then stood. With renewed determination, he approached the shield's edge and planted his feet in place. A group of four men stood eagerly to his far right with a look of anticipation as they watched the shield and waited for the opportunity to run at it. They smiled at each other and the crowd egged them on.

Benjamin cupped his hands adjacent to each other and created a small ball of light. It spun between them and he looked up at the shield. The men took up their running stances, but Benjamin did not toss it just yet. Closing his eyes, he included the light energies he'd come to feel throughout his lifetime, starting with the very first memory of his parents. He ran through every moment of his life he could remember—the good and the bad. There was so much bad, but he added it anyway.

The ball between his hands grew as it spun; it changed colors several times and sparks of lightning flashed out toward his hands. When he'd run through his entire lifetime, Benjamin opened his eyes. The ball was a golden sparkle of spinning light energy three times the size it had been before. He tossed it forward, and the men took off toward the shield. The ball hit the shield and illuminated it like cracked glass. The crowd gasped and cheered, looking on as the men were tossed more than twenty feet away. Benjamin looked at the jagged lines in the shield and walked up to it.

He ran his hand along the point of impact, and noted a tiny hole no bigger than a needle's point. He smiled and removed his finger. The color dissolved from the shield and Benjamin nodded. *More light; I need more energy.*

"You may break through it yet!" a male's voice proclaimed, pulling Benjamin out of his internal evaluation. He looked sharply to see a face he knew. The man standing before him was the one who challenged the guardian of souls so bravely, and was responsible for Benjamin's ease of acquiring the man he now called servant. He nodded, looking him over.

The man was roughly the same height and build as himself, but was of a much younger time. His clothing suggested he'd been traveling a great distance, and he wore a smile that warned Benjamin to keep both eyes open.

"So it seems."

"I would be more than happy to offer my assistance if you like," the man continued.

Benjamin raised a brow looking at him. "Your...assistance?" he repeated skeptically.

"Reuben's the name, and yes I imagine what ever you do could use a little boost," he said confidently. "With a bit of essence I'm sure you'll break through that barrier with ease."

"Essence?" Benjamin repeated, raising a brow, appearing a bit more confused than he probably should have knowing exactly what the man was referring to.

"Yes, it'll give a boost to whatever you are used to."

48

Benjamin doubted the sincerity of the man's words, having firsthand experience with this *essence*, and though he was sure it might help, what he needed, however, was more light energy. "And where do I find this…essence?" he asked.

"Well…." Reuben hesitated a moment, seemingly calculating as he tapped his chin. "In the great pools of wisdom, of course. But…you don't have to worry," he said, watching Benjamin's expression, "I have a system."

"A system?" Benjamin replied raising a brow. He was becoming bored with the man.

"Yes, an error-proof way to get what we want."

"And the guardians?"

"Leave that part to me; all you have to do is draw their attention with those lovely energy balls of yours, and I'll do the rest."

Benjamin was sure how that one would work out: A glimpse of himself running about tossing balls around just making the guardian angry while Reuben made off with the soul ran through his mind. He chuckled to himself—sure this man was up to something, but he considered it. *Access to the souls is all I need. The guardian will know the second I reach out, but I am better equipped to handle their abilities now, and a few seconds is all I need.*

"Sure, Reuben, we'll give it a try. Who knows, you may be on to something." He gestured toward the direction of the nearest pool and waited for Reuben to take the lead.

*

Tzofiya laughed so hard she snorted at the huge cat's words. She took a few breaths to compose herself before speaking.

"You know, for a wise one, you have a pretty morbid sense of humor, Kefirah." The panther snorted. "I imagine the humor of an archangel is not much different, considering we've many of the same stories to tell."

Tzofiya chuckled dryly. "I gather, and it's simply elder now. Perhaps one day when my duties have changed I shall again wear the title, but for now it's just elder."

The huge cat nudged her arm as they sat together under an ash tree. They were in the heart of the knowledge field watching the souls cross over. Tzofiya wore a pair of brown trousers and dark brown boots. Her form-fitting cream blouse was complimented with a dark brown scarf about her neck. Her hair was pulled back and braided with a very large cream-colored thong. At her hip was her sword; she had a row of throwing knives secured to her upper thighs and a small shield on her back.

"I've seen no elder do what you can, lady, and you still have your wings. They're just a little more…compact now, which is what gives you more of an advantage, I think."

Tzofiya chuckled again. "As long as I can st—" She stopped talking abruptly and doubled over, screeching in pain. Her blades scratched the ground as she wriggled about. Ultimately, she worked herself into a fetal position and was still. She panted heavily.

"What is it, Tzofiya?" Kefirah asked, standing concerned. "Benjamin!" The huge cat hissed and looked around, her fangs spread out as she took in the scents around them. "The shield…he's penetrated it somehow." Kefirah hissed again. "Stay here lady, we have company. I shall be fine on my own."

Benjamin followed Reuben along the path, making a meal of his light snack. He tossed an apple core aside and smiled as Reuben looked back, an indication of his continued presence. He pulled out some berries and started to munch on them. It would take them a little while to walk the distance, but they would get there at some point, and there was no need to be hungry and tired when they reached their destination.

Roughly an hour later, Benjamin and Reuben came upon the realm of mind. They sat a while resting their feet, as it seemed there was a bit of a commotion about the fields. Benjamin didn't pay much attention to it and was sure it would be over soon. He sighed as he sat back, leaning on one of several large stones placed about by the locals who feared the guardians and needed the landmark to stay clear of their fields.

Reuben built a small fire and started messing about in his things. Benjamin stared into the flames, watching the crackle of wood and twigs. Its warmth energized him. He smiled thinking of how something so small could affect him so much. Closing his eyes, Benjamin let the warmth radiate through him. The walk had taken a bit longer than he anticipated and the sun was starting to set. He could sense the hounds mobilizing and wondered why he was still getting warmer. The fire wasn't *that big*, but the feeling of warmth spread through him and kept growing, rising like an old friend's embrace. Benjamin quickly opened his eyes and looked around.

His eyes were glued on the slender creature fighting alongside the humongous panther as they faced over a dozen men.

51

She moved gracefully, effortlessly as she fought and although she didn't seem to need it, the cat was more protective of her than the souls it was tasked with guarding. Benjamin focused now as she moved through the air, twisting and twirling about, most of her time spent leaping off the ground; yet every strike was landed.

She tossed a few knives at one who got a little too close to the souls; Benjamin gasped as she then landed a fatal strike to another, her movements requiring her to turn completely around, revealing her features to him. Benjamin vaguely noted Reuben messing about by the fire; he'd taken to adding odd things to it. More than twigs and leaves, he'd tossed in some red sand, a handful of shells, and what looked like the last bit in a bottle of essence.

"The deal's off," Benjamin grumbled catching himself. He stood and slowly started walking toward the commotion. As he neared the grounds and the last intruder fell, Benjamin could not help but offer a smile as he looked at Tzofiya. It was her... She didn't have her wings and he wondered what happened to them, but it *was her*. She spared only a friendly glance his way before diverting her attention behind him. Benjamin lowered his brows and turned slightly, doing so in time to see a massive cloud of swirling gray race past him. It landed on both the guardian and Tzofiya. She'd taken a position in front of the huge panther and maneuvered her shield partly in front of herself in time for it to absorb most of the blow.

Tzofiya fell back grunting, and Benjamin gasped. Before he could react, another blast flew past him, hitting the guardian head on. Tzofiya groaned and tried to get up. Benjamin was at her side in a flash, reaching out to her as they were both hit full on by another burst. Benjamin flew through the air in one direction, and Tzofiya flew back, slamming into the ground hard. A low moan escaped her, and she was still.

Every part of Benjamin stung. He blinked a few times and could see Reuben moving toward him. His entire body was ablaze. The very core of Reuben was a deep red, and the farther away from his core, the fire's intensity was a bit less. Benjamin wondered briefly how Reuben did it, but did not waste time on the consideration as he saw Tzofiya laying still on the ground. He tried to get up, but Reuben placed a finger on his head. Oddly, it forced him back down. The spot where he'd touched Benjamin hurt worse than anything he'd ever felt before in his life.

"Stay, son of Adam." Benjamin lowered his brows.

"We have unfinished business you and I." He turned toward the guardian and slowly made his way to the panther that was now lying on its side, working desperately to simply catch a breath. It hissed at him, but otherwise stayed still.

"You!" Reuben taunted as he moved closer, sparing only a glance at the woman. "Your kind has taken from me, and I have come to claim that which is rightfully mine."

The guardian hissed louder, making her fangs as large and threatening as she could. She looked toward the fields a moment and her eyes grew wide as Reuben placed a hand on her snout. A deep rumbling hiss escaped her, and then withdrew as her body stilled. Her eyes closed, and her body became a sparkle of dust that swirled upward until it disappeared into the ethers.

The blaze was slightly diminished around Reuben now; his core looked more orange than deep red, and he staggered while removing his hand from the cat's snout. Benjamin frowned, looking on in amazement and frustration as he inwardly demanded his limbs to obey while trying to stand. Tzofiya moaned as she stirred and Reuben turned his attention toward her.

Benjamin growled and slowly made his way to his feet. Reuben turned and tossed a much smaller, less formed cloud at him. He wobbled a bit but stayed on his feet as the cloud hit his shield. Reuben lowered his brows and growled, watching him, then tossed another cloud at him, then another, and another came after that. Benjamin grunted and was pushed back slightly with every blow but was more secure in his footing now, and shifted more energy to his shield. He smiled at Reuben, who growled and leaped for Benjamin's throat. Benjamin sent a wave of blood energy through this shield and Reuben screeched in pain, releasing his efforts and pulling his hands back.

He grumbled to himself a moment and looked at Tzofiya, who was staggering to her feet. Frustrated, Reuben reached out a hand toward her, his flames all but burned out now, and Benjamin pulled on his light. It was dull, almost non-existent, as if he were created by something rather than born of the universe. Reuben only grunted and released a tiny cloud at Tzofiya before collapsing onto the ground, completely burned out of flames. Several of Benjamin's hounds raced forward and pulled Reuben away. They wasted no time devouring what was left of him, and Benjamin turned his attention to

Tzofiya. She was motionless on the ground, and the rise and fall of her chest was slow and labored.

Benjamin reached out, taking Tzofiya's hand, and closed his eyes. He ignored the gentle pressure from her fingers and pulled on his own light. He sent a trickle of energy to her and instantly fell to his knees. Her need was vast, and he was weak. He could feel her light now. It was dim, very dim. He tried pushing more of his own light into her, but it wasn't enough. She burned through it before her spark could return fully.

Tzofiya whimpered, and Benjamin opened his eyes. Her hold on his hand was a little stronger, but he could see in her eyes that she was still fading.

"No, I will not lose you again."

A small smile covered her features and he heard her speaking directly to his mind: *Benjamin, my light, my love, I'm so sorry, but its time for me to go.*

"No!" Benjamin yelled, but her light continued to fade.

I will always love you, brother. She went silent then, but he could still feel her light.

"No," he repeated, wrapping her in his arms. "If they won't come to you, I'll take you to them." He opened his eyes and looked out into the field of souls.

Anger rushed through him, and though he needed only a few, he pulled on the light of each and every one of them. The lights of billions of souls filled him. Their energy rushed through him like a furnace, and he began to glow. Benjamin pulled, not caring for the many voices that cried out in his mind. He tossed up a shield and

55

pulled more of their light. He took on so much that he was beginning to glow brighter with every passing moment.

When he could hold no more, Benjamin pulled back on the souls, but did not release any of them. He pulled Tzofiya closer to him and poured his light into her; he bathed in her presence again and smiled when he heard her speak.

"Benjamin, no," she whispered. It was small, but something. He could feel her light getting stronger, more powerful with every breath. When she squeezed his hand more forcefully this time, he smiled and gently released the flow of energy to her.

He opened his eyes and looked at her, exhaling. "You frightened me; please don't ever do that again."

Tzofiya offered a half smile as she tried to untangle herself from his grip. Her brows lowered as she looked around.

"Where are we?" she asked, rather surprised, looking more intently at their surroundings. Benjamin loosened his hold on her but did not let go.

It looked more like the mirrored pond where she'd saved his life so many years ago than the field of souls they were in.

"Could it be?" Benjamin asked, looking around. He could sense no barrier here, and the ever-present sound of approaching hounds not too far in the distance brought his attention back to her. He smiled. "It worked; we're in the realm of Adam, Tzofiya."

"But how…?"

"The barrier."

"The barrier could no longer hold him in place once he took on so many souls," came a familiar voice. They both looked up to

56

see Constantine standing there, battle ready with his sword drawn. He was at the head of seven archangels lined in a V. They too stood battle ready with weapons drawn.

Chapter Seven

DEATH BRINGER

"No!" Tzofiya yelled, an all-knowing look in her eyes. She drew nearer to Benjamin and tried desperately to hold on to him. He looked down at her and smiled.

"Don't worry love, I'll be fine." Releasing his hold on her, Benjamin stood to face them, then he quickly looked back at Tzofiya, who lost her balance trying to stand as well. She was still weak.

"She was hurt, Constantine, and you all did *nothing* to save her."

"We're here, aren't we?" Constantine countered. "Step away from her and release the souls."

As Tzofiya tried again to stand, she paused hearing Constantine's words, looked up at Benjamin, and lowered her brows.

"She's fine," he said, moving slightly to the side. "She just needs to rest."

"With your poisoned light coursing through her, I'm sure she needs more than that." Without another word, Constantine tossed a small blade at Tzofiya. It landed in-between her breast, and quicker than a thought, he was standing over her. Constantine knelt and put more pressure on the blade, driving it deeper into her body.

"I'm sorry, my love," he said looking into her eyes, "but this is the only way."

"No…" she whispered, tears streaming down her cheeks. She closed her eyes, and her arms fell limp.

"*No!*" Benjamin screamed. He ran toward Tzofiya, tossing out a wave of blood energy that sent every one of them flying back. He reached her side in a flash and dove into her presence, reaching, searching, and pulling. *Her light has to be here somewhere*, he reasoned; *she's so strong. Stronger than anyone I've ever come across.* He paused a moment as he came upon it.

"So weak," he said aloud, and sent every ounce of light he still held into her. He didn't care what was going on about him, though he could hear the angels moving about. *They must have recovered*, he reasoned, *no matter.* He tossed up a shield and shoved the remainder of light he still held at Tzofiya.

Benjamin, she said into his mind, *you'll be to weak; stop, its okay.*

He shook his head. *I don't care, I wont lose you again.* Benjamin immersed himself in her light, smiling as he felt her presence. *They can banish me to the edge of the universe if they like; as long as I have you I don't care.* Abruptly Benjamin went cold—ice cold. His hold on Tzofiya's light was gone, ripped away from him forcefully. He frowned and reached out for it again, frantic, but found nothing. Opening his eyes, Benjamin saw a golden spear spinning at the heart of the reformed archangels. It was suspended in mid-air, and glowing brightly. It was her. "Tzofiya," he said, reaching out to her. Standing, he dropped the shell that once held her light, and moved toward them.

Benjamin stopped at the pointy end of Constantine's sword and looked up into his eyes. "Nay brother," Constantine said, shaking his head, "she is no longer yours. Release the souls and I may let you live to mourn her." Benjamin growled and reached deep. He pulled on every single soul he still held, not caring at this point if they lived or died because if his actions. The angles cringed as if they too were affected and Constantine moved to strike. Stepping forward slightly, he twisted his hand and brought the sword around for a strike at Benjamin's neck.

Benjamin shifted his foot back and brought his arms around, arching them slightly as he formed a small energy ball. He released it at Constantine and sent him flying back nearly six feet into the air. Without a moment to breathe, he lifted his arms and moved them rather quickly to the left and to the right as he spun, shielding the attacks. He ducked and dodged the swords of angels, tossing balls of energy at them when he had the chance. Jumping and climbing was a necessary maneuver at times, but they each met his agility in turn. Benjamin had only a moment to pause as another archangel fell to the ground and rolled. His face was covered in dirt; he rushed for his sword and stood again, coming back for another chance at him.

Benjamin was growing tired of this battle as he caught another glimpse of Tzofiya's light glowing in the loosely formed circle the archangels held around her sphere. He grunted and pulled more light. His fatigue was becoming evident as his aim lacked its original accuracy. When he had the chance, Benjamin tossed a wave of light at them all, panting and gripping his knees as he watched them struggle to regain their footing. That brief moment however, was enough for him to move in close and reach out for Tzofiya's light.

"*Nay!*" Constantine screamed, running toward him. He extended a hand toward the spear, which had a slightly brighter glow now, and moved it. The spear moved just out of Benjamin's reach. Growling, Benjamin turned toward Constantine, pulling on and mixing together all the energies he felt. His eyes began to glow and he released a ball of light toward Constantine, who rolled out of the way, forcing the energy to be released on an unfortunate tree that exploded, causing debris to fly everywhere.

The angels all ducked and a few pieces bounced off Benjamin's shield. Constantine frowned and yelled something Benjamin could not make out. He blinked and raised a brow as the others all moved in toward him, swords at the ready. They were exhausted and Benjamin had had enough. He pulled forcefully on the souls' energy and felt the sting of several hundred souls as their lights were exhausted.

Benjamin stumbled to his knees, placing a hand out to stop himself from falling forward. He noticed that several of the archangels had as well. *They must be connected to the souls somehow,* he realized. He shivered as beads of sweat poured down his temples, chest, and back. The archangels encircled him, holding their swords horizontally. A ring of white light replaced the swords, and the angels spoke in unison.

"We banish you Benjamin, son of Lilith, to the…" is all Benjamin heard before he released the light patterns needed to form a gateway. His paradise awaited on the other side. All he needed to do was to step through it.

Smiling, Benjamin tried lifting his foot. It was stiff, heavy, almost frozen to the ground.

"We banish you, Benjamin, to the…." He grunted, pulling both light and blood energy together as he focused on his home. "…Realms of Samael, the realms of the deep and beyond. The…." Benjamin formed, pulled and shaped his ball of light. He looked past the bright ring at Tzofiya's sphere, and felt warmth flow through him.

In that moment, he released into it everything within him; Benjamin formed the ball of energy. not paying attention to the losses of souls he continued to feel. Not worried about what the angels were doing to him, not concerned with how he would get back to the realm of Adam, he just wanted his valley, his beast, and his home. A wave of green light exploded from the center of his energy ball. Simultaneously, the angels finished the last verse if their rhyme and the ring of white light moved toward him.

Benjamin closed his eyes and screamed at the top of his lungs: "My life, my souls, my realm!"

His skin burned and he moaned aloud. The light ran through him, pulling at his very core. Benjamin took his consciousness, his soul, his light, and wrapped it securely, along with every soul he still held, in a layer of protective shields. His eyes were sealed shut and he dreamed of Tzofiya.

When next he woke, everything was different. His speech was slurred, he smelled through a new nose, heard through new ears, touched with new hands, and moved with new limbs.

Everything around Benjamin was dead, and for miles around all he felt was the steady rise and fall of the hounds' lungs as they breathed in and out. He smiled, releasing his shields and letting the light of so many fill him. *Welcome back brother!* came a familiar voice. Benjamin looked around, seeing nothing, and heard a chuckle.

I am here brother, where you cannot attack me.

Samael? Benjamin sent back.

He chuckled again. *You really did a number on those archangels. I don't think they were out and about for at least five years.*

Years?! How much time has passed?

You've been asleep for nearly seven years brother.

Benjamin gasped.

Your light has touched the realm you stole in more ways than one. Many are gifted with light of their own now, which makes my job all the harder. He laughed.

What do you mean? Benjamin sent back, confused.

More often than not, beings are born there with more than average abilities, and the guardians have had no choice but to completely redesign the way they protect their charges.

Benjamin filled himself with more light from the souls he still held and smiled, releasing his pull to a gentle tug.

And what have they come up with?

Samael sighed and was quiet for a moment, then explained further: *Tzofiya's light was charged with the continued protection of the seven* realms. *There are others who help if they are strong enough to yield her light, and the presence of the wise ones is all but nonexistent now.*

Benjamin growled, *Then I shall take back that which is mine one realm at a time until I possess every part of her before leaving this realm forever.*

Samael chuckled. *Good luck, brother.*

Where does that leave us, Samael?

For starters, you need to find a way to get the souls you still possess from within my realms. It seems even in death they belong to you until you release them, and I need the space they are taking up around here. He laughed.

And next?

If ever you make it here, brother, you will hold an honored place in my realm as only Andlet-Beget can.

Benjamin stood and considered a moment, then repeated, *Andlet-Beget?*

Aye, the Death Bringer; never have I been graced with so many souls at once…however useless they may be to me. He laughed again.

"They will pay, brother," Benjamin vowed aloud, "every single one of them."

Benjamin's thoughts were once again his own, and he stood. "Andlet-Beget," he repeated smiling as he considered. "Ssso I ssshall be." He called forth his servants, and set out to find the light of the only love he had ever known.

End of Scroll 1

AFTERWORD

Thank you so very much for taking the time to read this work. Please take a moment to rate it.

For your time, I'd like to share a brief preview of what's next in this adventure...

Guardians of the Seventh Realm

"Don't you think he's a bit young for that?" the woman asked, admiring her baby as he sat among the pile of blankets, chewing on the gold chain that held a round pendant.

There was a faint glow coming from its center, and the wood crackled in the fireplace.

"He isn't that much younger than I was the first time I held it," the man said, wrapping his arms around her. He kissed her gently on the neck. She smiled. "Besides," he continued, "he should understand its connection early."

The woman, who stood about five-six with long black locks flowing down her back, turned to look at her husband. Her warm green eyes made him smile. He stood about five-nine with short brown hair and eyes.

"I agree, but perhaps it can wait until he's able to *hold* it properly."

"Sure." He laughed. "But then what would we use to teethe him with?"

They both chuckled as they looked on. The castle floors were cold, but the fireplace warmed the room. There were two large sitting chairs adjacent to the fireplace and on ether side of the blankets.

On the opposite end of the wall, a small wooden table sat holding a candle. As they turned for the chairs, a knock on the door followed by a request to enter redirected the male. He smiled at his wife in recognition of the voice on the other side. The woman returned the smile, and walked over to the child.

"Yes, Rhe? I expect you have a fiercely important reason for interrupting my evening." He chuckled slightly as he opened the door.

"Yes mi'lord...may I come in?"

The man's brows lowered slightly as he took in Rhe's expression of horror. He looked at his wife briefly before stepping aside to let him in. Rhe was of similar height and build as the man, but had dark red hair and gray eyes. The condition of his armor suggested he'd been in some kind of a struggle. The sheathed sword at his hip indicated that the struggle was not serious enough for the expression he wore, which only made the man more curious.

"My apologies, mi'lord," Rhe said, bowing deeply.

The woman reached down to pick up her baby, then looked to Rhe for his explanation.

"The castle walls…" Rhe began, then dropped to his knees suddenly, and wrapped his arms around his midsection, screeching in pain. The man reached out to him, but Rhe shuffled back slightly. The man's brows lowered, and he reached out again cautiously this time, only lightly placing a hand on his shoulder.

"Rhe, what's going on?"

After a moment, Rhe was still. Only his shoulders moved as he breathed in and out. He looked up, smiling crookedly. The man's eyes widened, and he swiftly removed his hand from Rhe's shoulder and backed away slowly.

Rhe laughed tauntingly. "I didn't think it would be this easy," he said in a deep, husky voice.

The man looked at his wife, who held their child close to her bosom. She closed her eyes and disappeared in a flash of bright white light. Rhe's eyes turned red as he looked on and noticed that the baby was holding the pendant.

"No!" he yelled, reaching for the woman, but he was too late. He turned to the man, who then asked angrily, "What…have you done…with Rhe?"

As if in response to his question, Rhe's lifeless body fell to the ground, his expression frozen in fear. In his place stood a creature more than seven feet tall. His skin was tan, and pulled tightly over his massive frame. Large claws rested where feet should have been. The sides of his legs were covered in thin white hair. His hands were large claws tipped with massive black nails. There was a second set of arms folded across his waist that were somewhat concealed under the black cloak he wore.

His attempt at following the woman made the hood of his cloak fall off, revealing the face only a mother could love. It looked rodent-like, hairless for the most part, and had the ears of a wolf. On his head and neck was long thinning white hair. His tan scalp outlined his scull. The red in his eyes seemed to glow as he turned to face the man questioning him.

"Hallll...varrr...durrr..." the creature said in a sluggish voice. "Your blood cannot escape me, nor can you defeat me without your tal...issss...man. What do you hope to accomplish by thisss?"

Hallvardr stood staring at the lifeless body of his friend and loyal protector. In his hand appeared a sward, the blade had a faint orange glow, and its guard was composed of twin dragons that curved up and around a black onyx pommel.

"Talisman or not, Andlat-Beget," Hallvardr said lifting the sword, "you have seen your last day."

"I do not think ssso," he replied harshly, then bent his knees and sprang straight up, disappearing and leaving a diamond-shaped void in the spot were he'd been.

"Oh no you don't," Hallvardr said keeping an eye on the darkness behind the shape. He jumped into it mere seconds before it disappeared, and emerged in a wooded area.

Following Andlat-Beget, he came to a clearing and froze. The outlined trees had disfigured bodies tied to them. The sent of blood filled the air and was muted only by the stench of death. Some of the figures were still leaking blood. Hallvardr could see what must have been human bodies at one point. On one of the trees, a pair of hands was clinched together.

In the center of the clearing, the stump of an aged cedar had a hexagram carved in its center. In between the points were six talisman keys. Only the center was missing.

"The seventh key," Hallvardr said mechanically.

He glad that his son had the other, then angered at the sight in front of him. True to his name, Andlat-Beget had come, and now he controlled six of the seven keys to the gateway.

Only in death would he have gained control over those keys, and death was all around him. Anger overwhelmed Hallvardr. He charged forward, raising his sword high. It glistened a sunset orange color and he drove it across the stump with blinding speed. Just before it touched the symbol, Andlat-Beget stretched his hand forth and a stream of white smoke left his claws. It landed on and around the stump, freezing it in place. The dragons forming its guard twisted swiftly and began crawling downward, but Andlat-Beget froze them as well.

He lifted his hand toward Hallvardr and unleashed a ball of green light so fast that Hallvardr had only time to acknowledge it before he was struck. He was violently flung across the clearing. The impact left him struggling to regain his bearings.

"Impressive, isn't it?" Andlat-Beget said, walking toward him slowly.

He reached out a hand toward the sword, then retracted it quickly grunting. His attempt at removing it left his claws charred. Hallvardr blinked several times.

His control of the keys is prime evil. Many will die if he succeeds in his venture here, Hallvardr realized. He was struck again as he tried to get to his feet, and suddenly knew how the others were bested. His eyes narrowed as he considered, *He must have combined the elements before addressing the guardians. This cannot be. He must be stopped.*

I know my love. I will find you, he heard his wife think.

Fear overwhelmed Hallvardr as he came to the realization that she would not be able to ignore this danger to the realm.

Annalisa would be in just as much danger as he.

"No!" he shouted, getting to his feet.

Before Andlat-Beget could fire another energy burst, Hallvardr released a stream of red-orange balls from his hands so fast that Andlat-Beget found it impossible to stay on his feet. It was a mistake, he knew it, but he would not lose his family. He pushed harder, desperately trying to penetrate the green shield Andlat-Beget threw over himself. With every burst he exalted, Hallvardr was weakened. Andlat-Beget had only to wait.

When he fell to his knees exhausted, Andlat-Beget dropped his shield, laughing. "I am disss…appointed. Your station demandsss…better of you. Perhaps with your tal…iss…man, you could have bes…ted me."

Hallvardr looked at the stump, thoughtful. After a moment, he released one last ball in its direction and fell to the ground, exhausted. Andlat-Beget destroyed it with a ball of his own. In front of his chest, a small green energy ball was turning. With each rotation, it grew.

"I will find your tal…iss…man," he taunted, "and I will bleed your key dry to open the gateway. I will use the still-beating heart of your blood to take back the light and reclaim this realm."

When the energy mass was roughly the size of a beach ball, Andlat-Beget released it straight for Hallvardr's heart. Before completing its mission, however, the ball was redirected by a beam of bright light directly in front of Hallvardr. The diversion sent it slamming into the stump, freeing the dragons, which then continued their decent. They blew fire upon the symbol, burning the wood it consumed.

As it crumbled under the fires demands, Hallvardr's sward broke through the symbol, effectively ending the spell. Two of the six talisman keys disappeared, and Andlat-Beget screamed in rage. He looked up to see Annalisa standing confidently in front of her husband, crimson staff in hand. His anger subsided slightly when he noticed the pendant hanging from her neck. He smiled and was further elated by the confusion in her eyes as she tried to teleport unsuccessfully.

Growling, Andlet-Beget threw a white ball of energy at her, yet it bounced away as if shielded. She bent to help Hallvardr up and hurried him through the nearby trees.

After a half mile, they stopped and she tried several times more to open a gateway, but each attempt was less impressive than the last.

"He still has four keys, my love," Hallvardr said weakly. "He cannot gain control of yours; the others will come willingly."

"You need your talisman," she responded, trying again to open a gateway, frustration clear in her voice. Hallvardr placed a hand on her arm and motioned his disagreement.

Sighing, Annalisa placed her staff down, closed her eyes, and reached deeply within herself. When she opened them again, a rush of wind ran down the length of her body, carrying a light crimson mist. When it reached the ground, it continued outward with blinding speed, and after five hundred yards it stopped, blowing away every last branch, leaf, and flower lying dead within its path.

Annalisa looked into her husband's eyes. They could hear Andlat-Beget's hoards approaching; they seemed to be coming from everywhere, beastly creatures just as hideous as their master. But none would cross the threshold, not without his magic.

Annalisa smiled.

No! Hallvardr shouted without moving his lips. *You will be defenseless.*

She looked around, tried again unsuccessfully to open a gateway, and returned her attention to him.

We will be defenseless, she responded without speaking. *We are guardians, my love, we must defend the realms.*

A group of hoards rebounded off the shield from all sides.

Then we protect them both", Hallvardr said.

He grabbed her hands as she closed her eyes in concentration. After a moment, a diamond shape no bigger than her palm appeared in front of them. She could see bright lights on the other side. Without another word, she released the pendant and sent it through the gateway. In its place, she fashioned a crimson glass replica, kissed her now armed husband, and turned to face their pursuers, Andlat-Beget at the lead. Death came, but not quickly enough.

About the Author

Rose Sweetwater is a veteran, active duty spouse, student, and homemaker. She lives in Virginia with her husband and three boys thrilled to enjoy life as it comes, while sharing her passion for writing with the world. As a student of life and metaphysics, she has inspired many around her and will inspire you too.

Be blessed and thank you for your time....

www.ingramcontent.com/pod-product-compliance
Lightning Source LLC
Chambersburg PA
CBHW020621130626
46552CB00003B/1067